ALL ALONE AFTER SCHOOL

Muriel Stanek
Pictures by Ruth Rosner

Albert Whitman & Company, Niles, Illinois

To Chris and Anna
with love. M.S.
For Nora. R.R.

Library of Congress Cataloging in Publication Data

Stanek, Muriel.
All alone after school.

Summary: When his mother must take a job and can't
afford a babysitter, a young boy gradually develops con-
fidence about staying home alone after school.
1. Children's stories, American. [1. Self-reliance—
Fiction. 2. Mothers—Employment—Fiction] I. Rosner,
Ruth, ill. II. Title.
PZ7.S78637A1 1985   [E]   84-17243
ISBN 0-8075-0278-2 (lib. bdg.)

Every day after school,
my friend Andy goes to his
grandmother's house to stay.

And Sue goes to
her father's shop.

But I take care of myself.
I'm all alone after school.

I remember when Mom first told me
she got a job downtown.
"I hate to leave you alone, Josh," she said.
"But we need the money, and I won't be
earning enough to pay a sitter."

"I can handle it," I said.
But I worried a little.

Mom said, "Staying alone may not be
easy at first. If it's too hard for you,
we'll work out something else."

During the next few days, Mom helped me
get ready to be alone.

"Always keep the doors locked," she said.
"Don't let anyone in the house. And don't tell people
you're alone. If someone calls for me, tell them
I'm busy and take a message."

"I know, I know," I said.

"And stay away from the gas stove," she added.

Mom made a list of phone numbers I might need
and taped it to the wall.
Her work number was at the top.
Below it were numbers for Grandma, Aunt Mary,
and Mr. Miles, our neighbor.
The emergency number for fire and police was in red.
Mom helped me practice using it.

IMPORTANT NUMBERS

MOM'S WORK 555-0318
GRANDMA 555-1324
AUNT MARY 555-9351
MR. MILES 555-1022
EMERGENCY - 911

Then she showed me how to lock and unlock our front
door and gave me a new house key on a brass ring.
It was the first real key I ever had.
She gave Mr. Miles a key and her work number, too.
And I brought a note to my teacher telling her
how to reach Mom at her office.

The morning came when Mom had to go to work.
Neither of us could eat much breakfast.
I guess we were both a little worried
about how the first day would go.

Mom hugged me and said, "Call me as soon
as you get home. And do your homework."

"Okay," I promised.

"Keep this for good luck," said Mom.
She gave me a smooth, flat stone, white as snow.
"I like to hold it when I'm feeling scared.
Somehow it makes me feel brave."

I watched Mom as she hurried to catch the bus.
Then I walked to school holding the white stone in my hand.

Andy was waiting for me by the flagpole.
We always meet there.

"My mom went to work today," I told him.
"And I'll be alone after school."

"You're lucky, Josh," he said.
"No one will boss you around."

All day I looked forward to things I'd do at home by myself,
like watching TV and playing with my baseball cards.
I wondered if I would be lonesome or scared.
Now and then I touched my pocket to make sure
the good luck stone was still there.

It was raining hard when we came out of school.
Some people waited in cars for their children.
Others stood with umbrellas and raincoats.
Andy's grandmother was there,
and so was Sue's father.
Nobody waited for me.

The crossing guard said,
"Hurry, hurry, you'll be drenched."
I put my spelling paper under my cap
to keep it dry.
Then I ran the rest of the way home.

Carefully, I put the key in the door
and turned it. But the door didn't open.
I tried again. It still didn't open.
I knew Mr. Miles, next door, would help,
but I wanted to unlock the door myself.

The next time, I pushed hard. The door flew open,
and I went inside. The house was awfully quiet.

I locked the door fast.
Then I took off my wet clothes
and went straight to the phone to call Mom.

"You okay?" she asked.

"Sure," I answered,
"I got a hundred on my spelling test."

"Best news I've had all day," she said.
But we had to say good-bye because
she got another call.

I got out my baseball cards and
started playing with them.
Suddenly the front door bell rang.
I didn't answer it.
It rang again.

Peeking from behind the curtain,
I saw a man I didn't know.
He was pounding on the door.

Without making a sound, I sat on the floor
and rubbed my good luck stone.
A yellow paper slipped under the door.

It said there was a package for Mom.
She could pick it up at the post office.
Good, I thought, that's over.

I was hungry now. So I got some milk and cookies. Then I turned on the TV to watch a magic show.

Later I did my homework and played with my games.

Mom came home at five-thirty, not a minute
too soon for both of us. We hugged each other
a long time.

I showed her my spelling paper and my homework.
"Good for you!" Mom said.

"How did you like your first day alone?"

"It wasn't too bad," I answered.

Then I told her how the door stuck
and about the delivery man.
Mom kissed me and said, "I'm proud
of the way you handled things, Josh."

That was a long time ago.

I'm a whole year older now.

Most of the time I like being alone after school.

But once in a while, it's still hard.

When it thunders and lightnings,

I get scared and wish

Mom were here.

Sometimes I need to see Mom right away,
like the time Billy Schultz beat me up.

Mr. Miles put some ice on my face,
but I had to wait until Mom came home
to show her my black eye.

Once I was a pilgrim in our Thanksgiving play.
Mom didn't see me on the stage because she
had to work. But Grandma and Mr. Miles came
and took pictures of me.

Usually it's nice having the whole house
to myself after school.

It's easy to do my homework when it's quiet.
And I like talking to all my friends
on the telephone.

Being alone gives me a chance to do things
for myself and for Mom. And I like it.
I make my own bed, take out the garbage,
and set the table for supper.
Mom says I'm a big help.

On Tuesdays I go to Andy's house after school.
That's his mother's day off.
Mom picks me up after work.
Andy comes to our house on Saturdays
because my mom is home then.
Sometimes we play ball in the park,
if our moms know where we are.

Today a new girl, Becky, came to our class.
When it was time to go home, she looked scared.
"What's the matter?" I asked.

"My mom and dad both work," she said.
"I have to stay alone."

"Got your key?" I asked.

Becky pulled up a key on a string
around her neck. "I keep it hidden
under my shirt," she said, "so that
people won't know I'm alone."

"Where do you live?" I asked.

"Over that way," she pointed.
We walked together.

I waited until she opened the door.
"Call your mom," I told her.

"Okay," she answered.

I took the smooth, white stone out of my pocket. "Here," I said. "Hold this for good luck. It might help if you feel scared."

"Thanks," said Becky. "I'll give it back to you tomorrow."

"Keep it as long as you want," I told her. "I don't need it any more."